The Cats in the Classroom

The Sequel to

The Cat at the Door and Other Stories to Live By

Anne D. Mather
and
Louise B. Weldon

Illustrated by Lyn Martin

Hazelden
Center City, Minnesota 55012-0176

Library of Congress Cataloging-in-Publication Data
Mather, Anne D.
The cats in the classroom/Anne D. Mather and Louise B. Weldon; illustrated
by Lyn Martin.
p.   cm.
"The sequel to the cat at the door and other stories to live by."
ISBN 1-56838-086-0
1. Conduct of life—Juvenile literature. 2. Affirmations—Juvenile literature.
I. Weldon, Louise B.   II. Title.
BJ1581.M394   1995
170¹ .83—dc20   95-20369
                                                      CIP
                                                       AC

Editor's note
    Hazelden offers a variety of information on chemical dependency and
related areas. Our publications do not necessarily represent Hazelden's pro-
grams, nor do they officially speak for any Twelve Step organization.

To our mothers
Virginia W. Bishop and
Millie M. Mather

Contents

About the book:

The Cats in the Classroom is a collection of stories that teach children by example. The children in these stories face common childhood situations—getting braces, name-calling, teachers' pets, embarrassing moments, and family problems. Through their experiences, they learn rich life lessons. They learn about the value of friendship, honesty, forgiveness; the importance of trusting your instincts, sharing your feelings, standing up for your beliefs; and the joy of family togetherness, nature, laughter. Most important, they learn to like themselves.

For parents who are trying to teach their children values but are not sure how to explain abstract concepts, *The Cats in the Classroom* at once offers the guidance of an inspirational book but the appeal of an illustrated storybook. Children will enjoy reading the stories on their own but will also benefit from discussing them with their parents. It is a book for the whole family to live by.

About the authors:

Anne D. Mather is the co-author of *The Cat at the Door and Other Stories to Live By.* She has been a professional writer for twenty years. She works for the Centers for Disease Control and Prevention, and the Task Force for Child Survival and Development. She has written extensively on addiction issues and is the author of *Bridging the Gap,* a guide for teenagers.

Louise B. Weldon is the co-author of *The Cat at the Door and Other Stories to Live By.* She is the coordinator of the Child Abuse Prevention Program with the Woodstock Police Department. She teaches parenting classes and self-esteem classes through the continuing education departments of DeKalb and Kennesaw State Colleges. Ms. Weldon is a frequent speaker on children's issues for seminars, civic groups, and church organizations.

Acknowledgments

We would like to thank everyone who has made our first book, *The Cat at the Door and Other Stories to Live By,* Hazelden's number one children's book. We particularly want to thank the following people for their love and support: Guy Bishop; Glenda Cannon; Sue Dean; Joe Dominguez; Rose Mary Hatfield; Vince Hyman; Brian, Jeannie, and Maggie Kelly; Kappy Lord; Kris and Linda Mather; Carol Maxwell; Ray McCants; Denton O'Dell; Susan Pilgrim; Jim Pittman; Rainbow and John Weldon.

Special appreciation goes to our friends at Hazelden: Sid Farrar, Leslie Johnson-Bryne, Rebecca Post, and Bobbi Rix.

Cat Problems

The Kelly family had cat problems—two of them. One was a golden-haired male named Rascal, the other a swaybacked female tabby named Angel.

The problem was that the family needed to move out of the house for a while. Ten-year-old Jeannie just couldn't handle the winter chill that set into their lakeside cabin. She kept getting sick. So they were moving into an apartment until spring. But its owner was very firm: no pets. What could they do with the cats?

Mom and Dad called every cat-lover they knew, but they all had cats coming out of their ears already. The family considered boarding the cats, but that was expensive. Also, Jeannie and her sister Maggie couldn't imagine the cats in cages. Mom even put an ad in the paper: "Cat-sitter Wanted!" No result.

One night Mom told the children, "There is a solution to every problem, including this one. But we need your help. I know you kids can find a place for your cats. Please help us."

Maggie and Jeannie talked about it that night. It was such a big responsibility, to help their parents and their pets. But they felt a thrill, a feeling that because they had been asked to help, they would find an answer.

Positive thought: When I am asked to do more than I think I can do, something inside me says "yes."

Believing

At first, Jeannie and Maggie had no more luck finding a home for their cats than Mom and Dad did. The girls considered letting the cats stay alone at the cabin and checking on them once in a while. Then they remembered the time they had left the cats on their own for four days. What a mess! The house smelled like a barnyard, and two side tables had been overturned.

"No, that won't do," said Jeannie, furrowing her brow.

"Let's ask some of our friends at school if we could pay them to look in on our cats," said Maggie. But this didn't work either. Either the kids' parents didn't want the responsibility, or Maggie and Jeannie's lakeside cabin was too far away from their friends' homes.

"I'm really getting scared about this, Maggie," Jeannie said one night. "It seems like this problem is too big to solve."

"We've got to believe that we can solve it," said Maggie, pulling her white down comforter up under her chin. "Our cats need us."

Positive thought: Sometimes all I can do is believe.

The Purr-fect Solution

The next morning, Maggie woke up with a start. The school! Why couldn't they keep their cats at school?

She jumped out of bed and ran to tell her parents. "Would you call the principal?" she asked them.

Her parents looked at each other and at the same time said, "No, you do it."

"Me?" squealed Maggie. She knew her friends said she had the "power of persuasion," but this was testing things a bit.

"Sure," said Dad. "You thought of the idea, and you know your principal better than we do. Why don't you talk to him about it?"

"You might want to rehearse what you say," said Mom. "Think of any objections he might have and what you'll say if he says no."

"We trust you to do as good a job as we would," added Dad. "After all, children can talk to adults about important matters."

Positive thought: I can talk to others about things that really matter to me.

Cats in the Classroom

Maggie skipped out the door of her school and all the way to the bright yellow school bus.

It worked! The principal had said Rascal and Angel could stay at the school! Maggie squeezed herself. She was so excited she wanted to scream.

The cats would be kept in the enclosed courtyard in the middle of the school, the principal had said. But there were rules.

"You'll have to come early every day to clean their kitty litter," the principal said. "And you'll need to check their food and water daily."

"Could Rascal and Angel ever come to class?" asked Maggie, squeezing her hands together. Boy, she was really pushing her luck.

"Well, your history class *does* have a unit on the Egyptians. If I remember my history right, they were the first to tame cats and make them pets. Maybe Rascal and Angel could be your guests that day," the principal said.

Maggie couldn't believe it. Her cats in the classroom! And the principal hadn't been hard to talk to at all. "Why, the hardest part was deciding to do it," she thought to herself.

Rascal and Angel at school. Maggie could just imagine them perched on her desk, their ears perked up, their eyes focused on

the teacher's every move. Then Maggie started laughing. More likely, they'd be the kind of students who sleep through each lesson—or are caught looking out the window!

Positive thought: I can find solutions to the problems in my life.

They Say

Eager to find out who their new teachers were, the girls huddled around the class lists posted on the front door of the school building.

"Oh no," Rhonda shrieked. "Mary Beth has Mrs. Yardley. They say she makes kids stay after school almost every day."

"They say she doesn't even like kids," Grace added.

Mary Beth felt almost sick to her stomach as she listened to her friends talk.

That evening she complained to her older brother Bill about her new fifth-grade teacher. She repeated what her friends had said and asked why a teacher would keep kids after school if she didn't like to be around them. Mary Beth and Bill laughed at the thought of that.

"Give your new teacher a chance," Bill urged. "Gossip about teachers isn't always true."

Then he told her about the time he'd had with a teacher with a mean reputation. Bill said he had felt like Mary Beth was feeling now. He had ended up liking the teacher and learning a lot too.

Positive thought: I form my own opinions of people.

Back to School

It was the day before the first day of school, and the Bishop household was full of mixed emotions. One minute Jerry felt excited and the next minute he felt anxious. Sometimes he wasn't sure *what* he was actually feeling. He went outside to jump it all out on the trampoline.

Meanwhile, Jerry's older sister was talking to a good friend on the phone about how angry she was that she couldn't buy new brand-name jeans to wear on the first day of class.

In the kitchen, their little sister Denise was singing a song she had made up about being so glad to be a big girl who gets to go to kindergarten.

Each of the children was experiencing different feelings on this day. Some were happy feelings and some were not. The important thing was that the children were expressing their feelings in their own special ways by talking, singing, or exercising. They were not keeping them pent-up inside.

Positive thought: Expressing my feelings helps me deal with them better.

The First Day of School

It was the first day of school. As Lynn walked to class, she chatted with friends she hadn't seen all summer. Then she spotted Candy across the hall. She waved and gave Candy a big smile, but Candy just seemed to look right past Lynn.

"What's wrong?" Lynn asked herself. "Is Candy ignoring me? Did I do something to make her mad? Maybe she doesn't like me anymore."

"STOP IT!" Lynn muttered to herself under her breath. "I just have a case of the first-day-of-school jitters. I'm just feeling a little bit nervous. Candy probably didn't even see me. Or maybe she has her mind on her boyfriend. Or maybe, just maybe, her underwear is too tight!"

This picture made Lynn laugh. Feeling better, she smiled as she walked to art class.

Positive thought: When I feel good about myself, I view other people's reactions to me more positively.

Boredom

Nine-year-old Cameron Green was defining common words for an English assignment.

Boredom. He stared at the word. He knew how it felt—boring—but what was it, really?

Finally, he wrote, "Boredom is something between events. When I'm doing something I choose to do, I'm never bored."

Once again, Cameron—who wanted to be a writer when he grew up—noticed that writing something down made him realize something he hadn't known about himself.

"I never realized that being bored is a *choice* I make," he thought.

Positive thought: I can choose not to be bored.

Alike but Different

"Did you ever notice how some things that seem to look exactly alike really aren't, when you look at them closely?" Crystal asked her mom one day.

"Like snowflakes?" Mom asked.

"Yes, and twins. We have twins in my school, and the first day I couldn't tell them apart. Now they don't even have to be together for me to know who's who. They're really different people," Crystal said.

"Trees seemed all the same to me before I got interested in nature," said Mom. "After all, they all have leaves, trunks, and limbs. But now when I walk through a forest, all the different varieties amaze me."

"I guess we're all supposed to be different, Mom," said Crystal. "Or else we'd all be the same."

Positive thought: I'm like other people—but different too.

Braces

Gabriella had done everything she could to get ready for braces. She knew why she needed them—to straighten her teeth and to look better.

It didn't matter. She grinned at the mirror. All that shiny stuff in her mouth. Yuck!

It could have been worse. Mom had said that when she was young, hardly anybody had braces. Wearing them at that time made you the butt of awful jokes. But nowadays, half the kids in Gabriella's class had braces—goodness, they were almost a status symbol today!

But they weren't a status symbol to Gabriella.

At breakfast, she said, "Mom and Dad, I don't like these braces."

"But—" Mom and Dad both started to say something, but Gabriella held up her hand.

"I'm not saying I'm not grateful. I know they cost a lot. And I know they're good for me. You don't have to say anything. I just want you to know, I don't like them. I know I've got to wear them, but I don't like them."

Positive thought: I may have to accept some things in my life that I don't like.

The Bambi Principle

"I hate math," Bret said, bouncing his pencil across his school desk. Mrs. Olsen, Bret's teacher, overheard him as she was walking down the aisles of school desks, checking the children's progress.

"Bret, what movie did we all see yesterday on our field trip?"

Bret didn't hesitate. "*Bambi*," he said, puzzled. What did Bambi and Thumper have to do with multiplication tables?

"Do you remember Bambi's mother's advice? 'If you can't say something nice, don't say anything at all.'"

"I wasn't saying anything mean about anybody," Bret protested. "You must have misunderstood me. I said I was no good at math—and I'm not."

Mrs. Olsen raised her eyebrows and cocked her head quizzically at the boy. "Bret, *you're* somebody. The Bambi principle is not just a rule for how you treat others—but how you treat yourself too."

Positive thought: I talk nicely to myself.

Divorce

One night, Cammie said to her parents, "Almost all my friends whose parents are divorced think *they* caused it."

Mom shook her head. "You know, don't you, that divorce experts say that's nonsense?"

Cammie nodded. "But I think kids feel that way anyway," she said.

"It must be hard for you to hear such sad feelings. I'm glad you opened up to me about it," Mom said. "I wonder if your friends wouldn't feel better if they told *their* parents their fears. I bet their parents would be relieved to set them straight."

Positive thought: I am not the cause of my parents' troubles.

Nobody's to Blame

Bennie, age nine, always blamed everybody else for his problems. If he didn't do well on a spelling test, it was because the teacher called the words out too softly. If he struck out during a game, it was because the team members were making too much noise for him to concentrate. If he couldn't find matching socks, it was his mom's fault.

Bennie's parents were concerned. They decided to look at their behavior to see if their son was learning some of this blaming from them. They asked Bennie to help them play detective.

They were astonished by their findings. When Dad made a mistake like spilling his coffee or cutting himself shaving, he would say, "Look at what you made me do!" to whoever was in the room.

And when Mom helped a neighborhood child up after the girl fell off her tricycle, she said, "Oh, bad tricycle. Look what you did to little Samantha." She was blaming the trike!

"Now I see where I got this blaming stuff—from you guys!" Bennie said with a twinkle in his eye.

"Looks like we've all got some changing to do," his mom said.

Positive thought: Accepting responsibility for my behavior helps me change it.

Back in the Blaming Habit

Bell's Ferry School was participating in the "Jump Rope for Heart" fundraiser for the Heart Association. The kids had two weeks to sign up on a team. Bennie went to sign up on the last day, but all the teams he wanted to be on had been filled.

"Blast that Tony," he thought. "He took the last space on the team I wanted. Now I'll have to be on a team with people I don't know."

"Whoa!" Bennie said to himself, almost out loud. "Stop blaming Tony. He didn't do this to me. If I had signed up earlier in the week, I could easily have gotten on the team I wanted."

Bennie realized how easy it was to slip into the blaming habit!

"I guess it will take more than one day to break this bad habit," he thought. "I'll do better next time."

Positive thought: I am gentle with myself as I change my habits.

Too Blunt

Mom went to a three-day meeting out of town. When she returned, she told the children a sad story. For the first few sessions, the conference leader had divided everybody into groups to work out different problems. But for the last get-together, the participants got to choose their own group of four people.

No one wanted to be in a group with one particular man.

"Why not?" asked Juanita.

"He was just too blunt," said Mom. "He said anything that was on his mind—and believe me, some of it was really negative."

"Like what?" asked Juanita.

"Oh, he told one woman that he didn't like the way she dressed, and he told one man that he talked too much. And he was always complaining about everything."

"Didn't you feel sorry for him when nobody wanted to have him in their group?" asked Juanita.

"Yes, I did," said Mom, "but not enough that I wanted him in ours. He just never learned to keep some of his bad thoughts to himself—so he ended up *by* himself."

Positive thought: I don't have to say everything I think.

Letting Bad Thoughts Go

Juanita was in the kitchen, shredding cheese for taco salad. Her mom was browning beef.

"Mom?" Juanita asked. "Yesterday you were talking about the man who couldn't keep his thoughts to himself. Well, what do you do if you don't want to keep a thought to yourself?"

"Are you talking about scary thoughts and feelings—like nightmares?" Mom asked.

"No, I mean nasty thoughts about someone. Sometimes I feel I hate somebody. I can't stand these types of thoughts, and it scares me when I get them."

"First of all, Juanita, everyone has had thoughts like those. Having an angry thought doesn't mean you're a bad person."

Juanita looked relieved.

"But still, it doesn't feel good to hate someone, does it?" Mom asked. Juanita shook her head.

"Well, you can refuse to have such ideas in your mind. Instead of being upset by them, just imagine that they're floating up and out of your body. You can even tell them good-bye if you want to."

Mom took the shredded cheese from Juanita, and added, "If that doesn't work, then talk to someone, okay?"

"Okay," agreed Juanita.

Positive thought: I can let go of bad thoughts.

A Get-in-Touch-with-Me Day

Molly had just gotten the craziest homework assignment! The teacher said tomorrow was "Get-in-Touch-with-Me Day." To prepare, Molly was to list ten things she liked about herself.

This was harder than it sounded. She couldn't just write, "I'm pretty," even though Molly really did kind of like the way she looked. What if the teacher made Molly read her list out loud? Her classmates would think she was conceited, and she'd be so embarrassed.

So instead Molly listed ten things she really liked to do. As she wrote them down, she got excited just thinking how much fun it was to talk for an hour with a girlfriend or to go fishing and feel the tug as a fish pulled her red-and-white bobber deep into the water.

Realizing what pleased Molly made her see just how wonderful life can be.

Positive thought: When I think about how many things I enjoy, I realize how good life is.

Teachers' Pets

Freckle-faced Casey tried hard in school, and he always liked his teachers. Once, when he had made a shoe box scene of Tom Sawyer, the teacher had even held it up for the whole class to see. Casey had thought he'd burst with pride.

But that was the exception, not the rule. Not like Marcie. For as long as Casey could remember, Marcie had been a teacher's pet. Teachers weren't supposed to show they had favorites, but Casey knew they did.

So it was with a sigh of relief that Casey heard one day at Sunday school that God doesn't play favorites.

"Life isn't a classroom, and God doesn't choose pets," said Casey's Sunday school teacher. "Each of us is special and important to God," he continued. "None of us is overlooked."

Positive thought: I am special and important.

Skipping Rocks and Cooking Spinach

The three girls got up early on the first weekend after school was out. They couldn't wait to walk around the edge of Lake Burton and skip rocks on the cold waters.

Over breakfast they reviewed the schedule for the day: going waterskiing, having a potluck dinner, and playing charades.

"Oops!" Rainbow said, remembering her promise to help prepare spinach puff. "I promised my mom I would make dinner," she told her friends. "And it takes a long time to get it ready. I hope we'll still have time to play outside after I'm finished."

"Let's all make it together," Jeannie piped in. "We can do it a lot quicker that way. Then we'll all have time to play."

Out came measuring cups, spoons, bowls, and ingredients.

Jeannie chopped the butter while Maggie grated two cups of cheese. Rainbow beat the eggs and supervised the cooking since she had made the recipe before. In a jiffy the ingredients were mixed and ready to pour into a casserole dish.

Working together on their project was such fun that the girls even cleaned up the dishes without complaining, and they had plenty of time left to play before dinner.

Positive thought: Working together allows more time for playing together.

Name-Calling

"I don't care if my grades drop," Sally sobbed to her school counselor. "I cannot wear these glasses in class. I hate them and the kids call me 'four eyes.' I'll catch up on my subjects at home at night. These glasses are not going to ruin my fifth-grade year."

Ms. Jacobs listened. Then she told Sally about a little mental game that has helped a lot of kids handle teasing.

"Imagine that you are sitting by a telephone that has several incoming lines," she said. "One of the lines is marked IGNORE. When someone calls you a name, picture yourself pressing the ignore button. The person will get very bored with no response from you and, after a while, will leave you alone."

Positive thought: Whenever someone calls me a mean name, I just press the ignore button.

Parents Like Kids

Twelve-year-old MacKenzie was hosting her aunt's baby shower. She handed her Aunt Rita the gifts and wrote down who had given what so her aunt could send thank-you notes later.

All the women were oohing and aahing over tiny T-shirts and baby booties. And they were telling stories about *their* children—not only as babies, but now.

MacKenzie heard about one child's talent at playing the piano. She learned that her cousin Ryan was always asking questions. Even though Ryan's mother said all his questions "drove her crazy," MacKenzie could tell by the way she talked that she was proud of her son.

Suddenly, MacKenzie realized how much parents talk about their kids and how proud they are of them. It had never really hit her before that parents *like* kids.

Positive thought: My parents not only love me but they also like me and are proud of me.

What a Relief!

When Jason woke up, it took a minute for his mind to catch up with the satisfied feeling he had. Then he remembered. Yesterday, his dad had agreed to go into an alcohol treatment center. The feeling Jason was having was a new one: relief.

No more drunk Dad at games. No more canceling sleepovers because Dad "wasn't himself." No more shame and secrecy. Shame that someone would know. Secrecy to make sure no one did.

Jason didn't have those feelings now. In the last few weeks, he had learned that his dad was not bad because he did bad things when he was drunk. His dad needed help.

Now Dad was in a hospital. Yesterday, Jason, his mom and grandparents, and even Dad's boss had talked to Dad in something called an "intervention." And it had worked. Dad wanted help. He said he had been feeling like he was going crazy.

Dad's relief had surprised Jason. He had expected anger— that's what always happened when he and Mom had tried to talk to Dad alone about his drinking.

But this time, with the whole family in the room determined to show Dad that he had a problem, and that they loved him enough to want him to get help, Dad had listened.

Positive thought: Sometimes it takes lots of love and lots of people to solve really big problems.

Hard-to-Express Feelings

Alicia's seventh-grade cousin Stephanie was really mixed up. Her parents had gotten a divorce, and because of that Stephanie had to move far away and switch schools. She was scared and angry. She had started cutting school.

Alicia's mom knew how much her daughter liked Stephanie. "Why don't you write her?" Mom suggested. "It would mean so much to her to hear from you."

But Alicia found it hard to know what to write. She felt she should say something, but she didn't know what. Then one day when she was browsing in a card shop, she saw a card that really reminded her of her cousin. Steph loved cats, and this card had a cat clinging to a branch, using only its front paws. Inside, the card read, "Hang in there."

Alicia bought the card. As she was reading it over, she grabbed her pen and wrote in her pretty, rounded handwriting: "I love you."

Alicia was learning a way to communicate hard-to-express feelings. Something inside her knew what to do, even in this hard situation, and she was learning to trust it.

Positive thought: I trust myself to express my love in the right way.

Her Story

"Once upon a time . . ." Those were Sarah's favorite words. They were the beginning of so many stories. The minute she heard them, she thought of dark forests and tall princes and pastel-colored castles.

But today, those words were to start a different story: *her* story. She was to write her autobiography for English class.

So Sarah started telling her story. She wrote about where she was born, how many brothers and sisters she had, and the exciting things that had happened to her, such as the time her family moved to Los Angeles not far from the stars' mansions.

But Sarah noticed that her story—unlike storybook ones—had a lot of loose ends. She didn't know yet what she would be when she grew up or even which teacher she'd get next year. She couldn't wrap up her story like a package with the tidy words, "The End."

Chewing her pencil, Sarah thought and thought how to end her autobiography. Finally she wrote, "I've had a lot of beginnings. But I'm in the middle of a lot of things and don't know the endings right now. *That* is my story."

Positive thought: It's okay to have uncertainties in my life. Everybody does.

The Sounding Board

Vinnie sat on the back porch petting his Labrador retriever, Spike. "You're the only one who loves me, Spike. I'm sure glad you are my friend," Vinnie said to his pet.

"This day has been awful," he confided to Spike. "I had a fight with my friend Seth and got in trouble with my teacher too. My little sister is getting on my nerves real bad, and I am totally bored. This ninety-degree weather doesn't help. It's too hot."

Spike panted heavily with his mouth open and his long tongue hanging out. He seemed to agree with his master.

"You look pretty hot, too, Spike," Vinnie said, scratching Spike's ears. "Let's go for a walk to our favorite place." Spike jumped up. He knew exactly where they were headed.

The pair ran down the stone path to the creek. Spike was splashing around in the water before Vinnie could even get his shoes off. They both got soaked.

On the walk home, Vinnie talked to Spike some more. "What I like best about you is that you always listen to my problems and never, never give me advice. You're a great sounding board even when I'm sounding bored. Thanks for being my buddy," he said as he patted Spike's wet, black head.

Positive thought: Sounding out my problems helps me to sort them out.

The Threat

"If you won't play the card game I want to play, I'll go home," Kendra said. She took the last sip of her orange juice and waited for Ladonna to give in, just like always.

Ladonna took a deep breath and said in a steady voice, "I don't want to play cards today. I want to play my new video game, and I wish you would play it with me. If you want to go home because I won't play cards, then I'll play the video game by myself."

"Sounds like you don't want to be friends anymore," Kendra said as she stomped out the back door in a huff.

Ladonna was afraid that would happen. It had been hard for her to say those words, although she had practiced.

As Ladonna stared out the window watching Kendra walk home, she felt many feelings. She felt courageous and happy that she had spoken up for herself. She also felt sad because she knew her friendship with Kendra might change.

Ladonna planned to call Kendra later and talk. "I'll tell her what I want," she thought to herself. "I want to stay friends, but our friendship has to have more give-and-take." She took another deep breath and sat down to play her new video game.

Positive thought: I have the courage to speak up for myself.

The Winning Point

"Uncle Bill, you're getting twice as many points as I am!" Buddy said as he carefully added the points and recorded the score. They were playing the new *Scrabble* game Buddy had gotten for his birthday.

Uncle Bill responded with a "hmmm," but his concentration did not leave the word he was trying to form with the seven letter squares.

Buddy noticed his uncle didn't seem to care whether he was winning or not. He wasn't rubbing it in at all. He just seemed to be enjoying himself.

Buddy began to try to make bigger words. He felt great when he added six letters to a word his uncle had already made. "Look, Uncle Bill. I made the word *sunflower*. I made a nine-letter word!" he exclaimed.

Buddy began to enjoy the game for the fun of it and not just for the score. And as he began to enjoy the game, a funny thing happened. His playing improved, and his score climbed.

Although Uncle Bill's score was higher than Buddy's at the end of the game, Buddy won, too, because he had learned how to have fun.

Positive thought: I am always a winner when I have fun.

Too Good to Be True

Louise could not contain herself. She was more than excited. She was ecstatic as she told her friend Ramon about her "A" in math and "A-plus" in English.

"This means I'll receive the Student Excellence Award this year!" she said. "And what's even better, Mandy invited me to her sleepover party Friday night. We're going to practice all weekend for cheerleading tryouts."

As the pitch of her voice got higher, she added, "Everything good is happening to me. It's just too good to be true!"

"No, it's not too good to be true, Louise," Ramon said. "All these good things *are* true. You deserve them and I hope you will enjoy every one of them."

Positive thought: I deserve all the good things in my life and I enjoy them.

A Listening Ear

Lucy was known as the "Dear Abby" of her block. She was always giving advice.

After a while, Lucy noticed that most people listened to her good advice but did what they wanted anyway. Like when Lucy told her brother Mike how to get along more with their dad. Watching the two of them in yet another argument, Lucy could see exactly what Mike was doing wrong. He wasn't listening. He was interrupting. And he had an "attitude." But when she gave Mike this good, free advice, he listened and then acted exactly the same way the next time. This made Lucy mad.

Once in a while, someone *would* follow Lucy's advice. But if things didn't work out well, Lucy felt guilty. This happened when Lucy decided to take shy, little Diana under her wing. Lucy decided that a new look was what Diana needed. So she lent Di her new hot-pink sundress.

Then a funny thing happened. When Lucy wore that dress, she felt like a model. But it seemed to make Diana even shyer. The girl retreated more and more behind that loud dress, like a turtle hiding in a big, pink shell. Lucy couldn't even think of this incident without shuddering.

Finally, Lucy decided to think twice before giving advice. She decided that knowing what would work best for her didn't mean she knew what would work best for other people.

She decided to listen to her friends—but to let them solve their own problems.

Positive thought: Instead of giving advice, I give a listening ear.

The Good Night Routine

Mrs. Mullinax tucked her girls in for the night, gave them each a big kiss, and said as she always did, "Just remember, God is watching over you."

"But I don't want God watching over me," said Ashley, the youngest girl.

Mrs. Mullinax smiled. She knew exactly what Ashley was thinking.

"Honey," she said, "God is not watching over you to see if you are doing something *wrong*. God is watching over you to keep you safe."

Little Ashley looked relieved as she drifted off to sleep.

Her older sister Misty smiled at their mom as she turned off the light.

Positive thought: God watches over me and keeps me safe.

Telling the Truth

"I was outside playing with a friend, and I lost track of time. I'm sorry I forgot about your game," Bo said to her best friend, Debbie, over the phone. "I hope I can come next week," she continued.

Mom, who was in earshot, smiled as she heard Bo talking.

"I'm proud of you for being honest," Mom said to Bo when she got off the phone.

"It was hard to tell Debbie I forgot about her game. I was a little embarrassed since we had talked about it on the bus coming home from school," Bo replied.

"I did consider telling her you couldn't give me a ride, but then I decided to just tell her what really happened. And she understood. She forgets things sometimes too," Bo laughed.

Positive thought: Being truthful helps me build better friendships.

Getting Away

Brian was driving Joey crazy. First, Brian had borrowed Joey's bike without asking. When Joey had told him not to do that, Brian told Joey he was stuck-up and selfish. To cap it all off, the next day on the school bus, Brian kept up his name-calling.

Joey thought of all the things he'd like to say to Brian, but decided he'd rather just get away from him. He was sick of nasty words. Brian just wasn't fun to be with, and Joey didn't feel like putting up with him anymore.

So Joey turned to Brian and said, "Brian, I'll see you later. Got to go." And he left.

Joey did something healthy for himself. He got his mind off something upsetting, and he got his body away from trouble.

Positive thought: I can turn away from unpleasant people and things.

When You Can't Get Away

Joey was pretty proud of himself for handling Brian by ignoring him. No fights. No mean words to have to clear up later. He felt good.

But a couple of days later, Joey found himself in a situation he wanted to just walk away from, but couldn't. Joey was at school, sitting at his desk, when he overheard a classmate saying something really mean about someone that Joey knew. Joey had no idea if what his classmate was saying was true or not. All he knew was, he didn't want to hear it.

But he couldn't just get up and leave. He was in school! So instead of "going someplace," Joey went inside himself for a few moments. He thought about being at Lake Rabun in the summer. He could just feel the warm dock on his stomach as he lay peering over the edge at the fish below. There was one big bass that always swished by so proudly. It was beautiful!

Joey got so involved in his mental fishing game that he forgot all about the gossip he hadn't wanted to hear.

Positive thought: I can move my thoughts from unpleasant thoughts to pleasant ones.

101 Spots

Tad arrived home at three o'clock from seeing *101 Dalmatians* at the movies. By five o'clock, with the help of a black magic marker, he had a Dalmatian of his own. The formerly white wirehaired terrier was now a polka-dotted dog. The pooch didn't seem to mind at all.

Tad proudly walked into the den to show his parents the new dog with 101 spots. The frown on Dad's face and the gasp from Mom clued Tad that his parents were not happy with his Dalmatian creation.

"What happened to Frosty?" Dad asked in an annoyed voice.

Seeing the marker in Tad's hand, Mom knew right away what had happened. She said, "I hope you used a washable marker! Those spots are going to be hard to get out."

Mom was right. Tad spent a long time that afternoon washing Frosty in hot, sudsy water. After he had gotten as much ink off as possible, Frosty's normally white coat still looked grey. The family then took Frosty to the grooming shop, and Tad spent a couple of weeks' allowance to have Frosty bathed again. The shop owner had to put a medicated rinse on Frosty to prevent skin irritation.

Tad decided to use paper—not pets—for his future artwork.

Positive thought: I'm glad I can correct some of my mistakes.

Making Choices

"Mom, I just can't stand it when Peter gets rude with me," said Josh. "Today he told me to move from my seat on the bus. He's so bossy."

"What did you do?" Mom asked.

"I didn't do *anything*. I was so mad, I just froze."

"That happens to me sometimes," Mom said. "Like the time one of your teachers 'volunteered' me to hold a fundraiser in front of a whole group of people! I could have screamed."

"Did you?" asked Josh.

"No," said Mom. "I froze too. But let's put our heads together and see what we *could* have done or said, instead of doing nothing."

"Well, I could have jumped up and down and screamed at Peter," said Josh, smiling at the thought. "That certainly would have gotten his attention. Or I could have just laughed. I'm not sure what Peter would have done if I'd just laughed at him."

"Those are two choices. Anything else?" she asked.

"Well, Mom, I guess I could have just said no," said Josh, a little sheepishly.

"Me too," said Mom, laughing. "I could have just said no, too."

Positive thought: I can choose how I react when someone is rude to me.

Them Bones

Colleen and her dad were working on her fourth-grade science homework. They were studying the human skeleton.

"There are 206 bones in the body," Colleen read aloud. "There are sixty just in my arms and hands! I can't believe it—you can't see even one of them!"

Reading on, Colleen learned that the skeleton holds up her body, gives it form, even makes it possible for her to walk and run.

"It's so weird that something you can't even see—your bones—are holding up something you *do* see," she told her dad.

"It's not really that strange," said her dad. "If you think about it, you can't see a lot of the most important things in your life: music, for example. Or peacefulness. Or joy."

Colleen thought for a minute. She just loved her older sister Katie. They were only ten months apart and almost like twins. A lot of times when something went wrong at school, just thinking about Katie made Colleen calm inside.

"Love's like that, Dad," Colleen said.

"It sure is," said Dad, giving her a big squeeze.

Positive thought: I cannot always see the things that are working to help me. But they are there.

Help from Friends

Sherry's dad was in a serious automobile accident. Because he was in the hospital for a long time, Sherry stayed with her aunt in another town for several months.

While she was at her aunt's, Sherry became a Brownie Scout, met some new friends, and joined a church group for kids her age. Her life looked pretty normal on the outside. But on the inside, Sherry ached to be back home with her mom and dad.

Monday afternoon at the end of the Brownie meeting, her leader asked if any of the girls had a problem they wanted to talk about.

"Boy, do I!" Sherry thought.

She had kept her problems to herself the whole time she had been at her aunt's. But today, when her leader asked if anyone had a problem, Sherry's emotions were right on the surface. She let her feelings of worry, fear, and homesickness spill out as she told the group of her situation.

Some of her Brownie friends were surprised that Sherry had so many problems because she was always smiling. One by one, Sherry's Brownie friends found ways to let her know they cared about her.

Positive thought: I share my feelings and allow my friends to comfort me.

Turkey Bowl

"Ten, twenty, thirty, hut!" six-year-old Mary Ann called out. Then she hiked the ball to her big cousin, Will. The game began. This was no ordinary football game. It was the Turkey Bowl—an annual family football game played each Thanksgiving Day. Teammates ranged in age from six to sixty years old.

The family played football all afternoon. Afterwards they went inside and made sandwiches from leftover turkey and ham. While sitting around the fire and eating, the family laughed about the game and talked about next year's game plans.

"Next year I get to be quarterback," Mary Ann announced.

"Okay," said Will, "but only if I get to carry you across the goal line!"

When it was time to go, Cousin Will carried an exhausted Mary Ann out to the car. "You know, Mom," Mary Ann said as she snuggled into a blanket in the backseat, "I love getting together on Thanksgiving." She yawned and pulled the blanket tight around her.

"It's a great day to be thankful," she said as the car's gentle motion rocked her to sleep.

Positive thought: I am thankful for my family and all the love we share.

Giving My Best

Gita's rabbi asked her to decorate the bulletin board at the synagogue hall for Chanukah.

Gita squirmed. "I'm not that good at crafts and stuff," she said. "Don't you want to get somebody better for the job?"

"Gita, I'm going to be frank with you," said her rabbi. "Anything you do will be better than what I could do. And I don't know who else to ask. You know, you don't have to be the best to do your best," he said.

"Well, if you put it that way," said Gita, "I'll be glad to do the best I can."

Positive thought: I don't have to be the best to give my best.

The "Nice" Me

Emily was walking in the park. She was in a huff. Her neighbor Frances had said something really nasty to her.

Emily was thinking of all the nice things she'd done for Frances, all the reasons she did not deserve to be treated this way. Then she started to think about getting even. "I could just stop being nice to Frances," Emily thought. "I could just treat her like she treats me."

Emily stopped short. "If I *act* like Frances, I'll *be* like Frances. And I don't want that," she thought.

"What do you want?" asked a little voice inside her.

Emily thought for a moment. "Right now, I just want to be me—the nice me. I want to get rid of these angry, mean feelings. I want to feel good again."

So Emily concentrated on relaxing. She felt the wind brush across her forehead, like her mom's hand pushing back her bangs. Slowly, she began to feel better.

Positive thought: I can get rid of mean feelings.

Forgive and Forget

Several items had been stolen from Lou Ann in the past week: first, the handmade friendship bracelets that her best friend had given her; then, her dollar for lunch money; now, her pineapple-orange juice box she brought for afternoon snack.

"There are really rotten people in this school," she thought to herself. "I'd like to catch and hurt whoever is stealing my stuff."

Lou Ann's Sunday school lesson helped her change her mind about the situation. She learned how forgiveness can break a chain of negative events.

That night before she went to sleep, Lou Ann said to herself, "I forgive whoever took my bracelets, my money, and my juice." She even thought of a few reasons why someone might have stolen her things, which helped her feel much better than wanting to hurt the thief.

For a few days Lou Ann felt better. Then the old feelings crept back. Her desire for the thief to get into trouble returned.

The following Sunday, Lou Ann's teacher told her that sometimes you have to forgive more than once to really forgive and get over the hurt.

"Oh, I get it," Lou Ann said. "I keep on forgiving until the bad thoughts about the person fade away. Then I know I'm over it."

Positive thought: I work at forgiving until it works for me.

Life Isn't Hard

One day, Paul asked his mom if she thought life was hard. He said he had heard this expression many times.

"Well," she said, "I guess I don't really think that it is. Here's why. Name something you think is really, really hard."

"Being in the Olympics," Paul said.

"Good example," Mom said. "You know your cousin Katie? She's been practicing gymnastics three days a week for years now. She's placed in the state and may well go on to the Junior Olympics. To us, that would be work. To her, it's fun."

"What about paying off a mortgage?" Paul asked. "That must be hard."

Mom laughed. "I didn't even know you *knew* that word," she said. "A mortgage means you're getting a chance to own your own home. And that's an American dream! It's a real goal for people, and goals are fun. What's hard is working hard and never seeing any results!"

Positive thought: Working hard at what you love is not hard work.

I Can Say Good-Bye

Shandra and Penny were next-door neighbors and on-again, off-again playmates. Many times, Shandra had thought that if they hadn't lived next to each other, they probably never would have been friends.

But because they saw each other so much, they knew they had to get along. So although they fought a lot, they made up a lot too.

But one day, Shandra decided that she was tired of the bickering and tired of acting as if it didn't matter. She was even tired of going through all the motions of making up again. Shandra decided this friendship was just more trouble than it was worth.

Shandra did not want Penny to be her enemy. She just didn't want to spend time with her anymore. So Shandra decided not to. She remembered the good times she had had with Penny and, in her mind, thanked Penny, wished her well, and said good-bye.

She remained kind and polite to Penny, but she started to spend more time alone and with other friends.

Positive thought: It's okay to stop liking someone.

Coincidences

"What does God sound like?" Jeremy asked his camp counselor. They were alone in the mess hall, rolling up sleeping bags for the camp-out that night.

"I've read that some people have actually heard God speak," Big Mike said. "But it's never happened to me. Still I feel as if God gets his messages across to me."

"How?" asked Jeremy.

"For me, God speaks not in words but in events that happen to me," Big Mike replied.

"I don't get what you mean," Jeremy said, plopping down on a sleeping bag and looking earnestly at his counselor.

"I'm amazed at how many times coincidences happen after I've prayed. Like once when I was a boy," Big Mike said, "my uncle had a bad drinking problem. It really upset me to see him acting drunk and foolish, so I prayed about it."

"What happened?" Jeremy asked.

"The next week my school had a guest speaker from a group called Alateen. He talked to us about alcoholism and living with a person who has that disease. Now some people would say that was just a coincidence. But I notice that coincidences happen a lot when I pray."

Positive thought: God may speak to me through events in my life.

Mom's View

"Big Mike, my camp counselor, says God speaks to him through coincidinks," Jeremy told his mom one day after he got back from camp. They were peeling potatoes at the sink to make french fries.

"I think you mean *coincidences,*" said Mom, smiling.

"Does that happen to you?" Jeremy asked.

"Yes," Mom said, nodding. "It happens all the time. Especially with other people. Haven't you ever had a friend say exactly what you needed to hear to feel better?" she asked.

"I guess so," said Jeremy. It sounded familiar, but he'd have to think about it a while to remember what and when.

"It happens to me a *lot* with you children," Mom said shyly.

"Really?" Jeremy asked. Was Mom saying that sometimes he was an answer to her prayers?

"Yup. Remember that day last week when I was carpooling and you noticed I was crying? I was feeling bad because I'd gotten upset with you both that morning."

"Yes. And I told you I'd be crabby sometimes, too, if I had to do everything you have to do," Jeremy recalled.

"Yes. That was exactly what I needed to hear to feel better."

Positive thought: I can be an answer to someone's prayer.

Jeremy's Discovery

Jeremy had been mulling over and over a problem he was having. It was like a tooth that was almost ready to fall out—he just couldn't quit fiddling with it.

The problem was this: He needed money, bad. His parents didn't seem to understand that chewing gum didn't cost a nickel anymore, and that a kid just needed some spending money. He had tried to talk his mom and dad into raising his allowance, but it was no go. And he was too young to get a *real* job. What could he do?

Before going to bed that night, Jeremy added his request for a job to his prayers of thanks for the good day. He tried to put his worries away for the night. Finally, he fell asleep.

The next day, he bolted out of bed. He had the answer! It was to go to others, his neighbors, and let *them* tell *him* what they needed—and he'd do the work. The answer was that *he'd* be the answer to other people's problems! Now that was a good job, if he ever heard of one.

Positive thought: I can receive answers to my prayers.

Jane's Philosophy

One night, Jane was describing things that she didn't like to her mom.

This time, it was about Jane's sister being a pest. And boys teasing Jane.

Jane and her mom talked a lot of things out. Sometimes her dad would peek around the door to Jane's bedroom and say, "You two solving the problems of the world again?"

"Sure, Dad," Jane would say, laughing. But she knew they really weren't. After years of late-night talks with her mom, Jane had formed her own philosophy about problems.

As she said to her mom one night, "Life is full of things you have to learn to live with. You might as well learn to live with them because—even if you don't—you *still* have to live with them."

Positive thought: Many things in life I can change. But I accept that there are some things in life that I just can't change.

49

The Christmas Note

Katrina carefully opened the little envelope. Inside was a note written on green stationery, decorated with small teddy bears.

"Dear Katrina," the note began. "I hope you have a Merry Christmas and a Happy New Year. I'm sorry I couldn't get you a present, but I'm glad you invited me to your party. Love, Rebecca." Under her name, Rebecca had drawn ten little hearts.

Katrina hugged the note and read it again. She knew Rebecca's dad had been laid off at the factory. Rebecca just didn't have any money to buy gifts, and Katrina imagined how sad that must have made Rebecca feel.

Katrina ran to her desk and got out her own blue stationery that was covered with a pattern of seashells. "Dear Rebecca," she wrote. "Thank you for the most special gift of all—your friendship. I know it will last longer than any present."

Then she carefully sealed the envelope, addressed and put a stamp on it, and ran out to her mailbox to mail it.

Positive thought: Friendship is the most valuable gift I can give anyone.

Giving and Receiving

Colorful wreaths, silver doves, and manger scenes decorated the cards on the Conseco's mantel. The family favorite was an elegant egret standing in a snowstorm. The message inside the card wished the family the warmest of holiday greetings.

Mom, Dad, and Miguel sat by the fire in the living room reading the cards.

"Why do people send us cards when we never send out any?" Miguel asked his parents.

"Because they want to share with us during the holiday season," Dad replied.

"But we never send cards. I don't see why they send them to us," Miguel persisted.

"People express love and thanks in different ways," Dad replied. "Throughout the year, our family does nice things for people. Receiving Christmas cards is one way those nice things come back to us."

Positive thought: The good I do comes back to me from many different sources and in many different forms.

Kwanzaa

Ten-year-old Jamal and his nine-year-old sister, Keisha, were so excited. It was December 26, the beginning of the Kwanzaa holiday. Although this African American holiday was started many years ago, this was the first time Jamal and Keisha's family was celebrating it.

Keisha had helped her mom arrange the table where they would gather every evening for seven days. On the table was a straw mat, which was to show how important tradition was. An ear of corn and a candleholder with seven candles were on the mat. Jamal and his dad had made the candleholder themselves from a piece of tree limb that had fallen into their yard.

With a hush, the children gathered at the table, and Dad lit the first candle.

"This candle stands for unity," said Dad, pointing to a candle. "This is an important idea for our culture and for our family. What do you think of when you think of unity?"

Keisha beamed. That was easy. When she thought of unity, she thought of her family, right now.

Positive thought: I enjoy my family's celebrations.

World Healing Day

December 31 is a very special day. It is World Healing Day. On this day, everyone is invited to take part in a world celebration.

For one hour, people from different countries, religions, and governments put aside their differences and pray for peace in the world.

What could children do for one hour that would help the world? Well, Beth decided to read favorite prayers and offer up any thoughts she had for world peace. George decided to be with his family—each member of his family was going to name wonderful things that had happened to them during the past year. And Marguerite decided to just lie quietly on her bed, stroking her dog, imagining all the world to be as much at peace as she was right now.

Each year, over one billion people are expected to be a part of World Healing Day. What a special way to welcome the New Year for our planet!

Positive thought: I can be part of the healing of the earth.

I Am Loved

One afternoon, Ms. Swain was driving her daughter and a neighbor's child home from day care. The two girls were chattering away in the backseat. Their voices were barely above a whisper, but Ms. Swain occasionally heard a word or two, such as *God . . . lie . . . love.*

Soon the question came. "Mama," Ginger asked, "does God love you if you tell a lie?"

"Of course!" Ms. Swain said. "God loves you no matter what you do or say. God *is* love."

"So God will never stop loving you even if you do something bad?" the girls persisted.

"That's right," said Mom.

"Thought so!" the girls replied happily.

Positive thought: God loves me all the time.

Happy Tears

When their performing group was called out, the tap dancers ran on stage to receive the second-place trophy. The silver sequins on their bright red costumes shimmered in the light as the girls jumped up and down and hugged one another.

These five girls had worked all year preparing for this national dance competition. They had choreographed their own dance and had selected the perfect costume for the performance.

As the winners were being photographed, other students from their dance school sat in the audience, clapping and cheering. Hilary noticed that Margo, one of the winners, was wiping tears from her eyes.

Hilary elbowed the friend sitting next to her and asked if Margo was upset because she hadn't won first place. "I think second place is a real honor in a competition this big," Hilary said.

"Margo's not crying because she's upset. She gets tears in her eyes when she wins too," her friend responded. "She calls them happy tears."

Positive thought: Tears aren't just for expressing sadness. I can have tears of happiness too.

Security Blankets

Nathanial came downstairs, dragging his blanket. He lay down and cuddled inside it in front of the TV.

Nat also brought his blanket with him to the stadium to watch the local high-school football games. And, of course, he slept with it each night.

One day Nat's older sister Andrea teased him about his blanket. When their mother overheard this, she set Andrea straight.

"Nat's blanket isn't just a thing to him. It's something that makes him feel safe. It makes him peaceful inside. I would think you would understand that. Isn't that how you feel when you play piano?"

"Yes," said Andrea. "But I don't carry my piano around with me everywhere!"

"Maybe you would if you could," her mother responded. "Instead, you carry the feeling. Nat is little and hasn't yet learned that he can have those safe feelings without his blanket. Until he does, we need to respect his way of protecting himself."

Positive thought: I protect myself and feel safe.

Just for Fun

Becky's mom stood in the living room doorway and listened as Becky played the piano. Her mother was happy that Becky was showing an interest in music.

"You seem to be enjoying that so much now, Becky," her mother said. "Wouldn't you like to take lessons again? That way, you could learn to play *perfectly.*"

"No, I wouldn't Mom," she replied. "I don't care about learning to do this perfectly. I am doing it just for fun."

Positive thought: I don't have to do everything perfectly. I can do some things just for fun.

Teaching Parents

"Listen to this," said Dad, looking up from his newsmagazine. "Somebody has actually figured out that children laugh about five hundred times a day! Can you believe that?"

"I'm not sure I laugh that often in a year," said Mom.

"Oh, sure you do," said Dad. "But now that I think of it, it's often the children who get us laughing."

"Like their mispronunciations of new words," said Mom. "Remember when Kelly called *furniture* 'furni*chair*?'"

"And Tom asked if apricots came from Aprica," said Dad, laughing at the memory. "I guess that's something the children really contribute to our lives—teaching us how to enjoy it."

Dad and Mom talked about this for a while. Kelly, sitting out of sight in the TV room, was all ears. Her parents said it wasn't that she and Tom were the family comedians or anything. It was just that, by being children, they naturally added a lot of fun to the house. Her parents liked that.

Positive thought: I can teach my parents important things.

Birthday Surprise

The big day finally arrived. Grandma was seventy years old and her family had planned a big surprise party for her. No coaxing was necessary to get the grandchildren to help with the tasks to get ready.

Each of the three grandchildren had duties to do during the party. Leah was to serve the punch. She wore a very dressy pink dress that almost matched the color of the punch. Greg was to greet people at the door. His best Sunday suit made him look very official. Ben, the youngest grandson, was assigned a very important job too. He was to keep watch and let everyone know when the guest of honor arrived.

When Grandma finally stepped through the door, her eyes sparkled with delight. A lifetime of friends and family stood to greet her, shouting, "Surprise!"

After the party, the three grandchildren gathered around Grandma on the sofa.

"Grandma Ginny," Leah said, "you sure have a lot of friends. I think it's fabulous that a hundred people came to your party."

Little Ben piped up, "Of course she has lots of friends. That's because she knows how to be a good friend."

Positive thought: Being a good friend helps me to have good friends.

The Cat's Meow

The Cohens' new cat was very unusual. When he was six months old, he had suffered a high fever. Felicia and her parents had stayed up with him all night, rocking him gently. Though the cat lived, his meow was changed completely. Now he gave a funny little trill, almost like the sound a spring frog makes. The fever had also affected his purr. Now you could hear it only if you put your head right up to his throat.

Ever since that awful night, Felicia felt even closer to her cat than before. She couldn't look at him without thinking of how she had rocked him in her arms all that night.

One day a new neighbor met Felicia's pet and said, "This cat sure is weird. I've never heard such noises from a cat."

"He's *not* weird," said Felicia, putting her hands on her hips. "He just has a lot of special features."

Now whenever anyone in the Cohen family notices something a little out of the ordinary in a person, they say, "I guess that's just their *special feature*."

Positive thought: We all have our own special features.

Card Games

Hannah and her brother, Jed, had a new sister—seventeen-year-old Louise from Denmark. She was a foreign exchange student. The whole family couldn't believe how well Louise fit into their household. She loved the pets. She liked vegetables but not fish, just like their family. And she loved to play cards.

Their favorite game was called nerts. This was a wild version of triple solitaire. Hands flew madly and hearts beat wildly during play. And sometimes, fights broke out.

"You cheated," Hannah would yell at her brother. "I had my jack on the pile first."

"Did not," Jed would say. Pretty soon they'd be squared off.

Every time this happened, Louise would say, "Stop it," holding her palms to her ears. Even though she was angry, Louise would speak in her soft, singsong voice that the children loved.

"This is a game. If you're going to fight, why bother to play it?" she would ask very seriously.

This happened many times. At first, Hannah and Jed had thought Louise was being silly. Didn't everyone bicker during games? Then they started to cut it out because they liked Louise and didn't want to upset her. And finally, one day, Hannah realized that she and Jed didn't fight during cards anymore—and that she was enjoying the game much more.

Positive thought: I can play without bickering.

Feeling Bad and Fixing It

Gus paced nervously outside the karate instructor's office. He fiddled with the yellow belt of his white uniform.

When the instructor got off the phone, Gus knocked on the door and asked if he could talk to him in private.

Gus's palms were sweating. He swallowed hard and handed Mr. Dean a wadded up, damp envelope full of quarters.

"Last week I was assigned to count the candy money, and I took this out before I gave you the total," Gus said in a barely audible voice. "I felt bad about it all week. I'm glad today finally got here."

"I appreciate your bringing the money back, Gus. I knew some money was missing, but I had no idea what had happened to it," Mr. Dean said.

Positive thought: Feeling bad about something I've done is a clue that I need to correct it.

Chill-Out Time

Jill made a conference phone call to two of her friends. They chatted away, making plans for the weekend. When Jill got off the phone, she told her mom about all she and her friends wanted to do that weekend—play goofy golf, go to the mall, and spend the night together. Jill also had a baby-sitting job Saturday evening.

Mom was a little concerned that Jill wanted to book her weekend so full. "If you make a schedule of how you'll get your chores done *and* have time to relax, maybe I'll let you do all those things," she told Jill.

Jill liked that idea. When she showed her schedule to Mom, her mother was curious to see something called "Chill-Out Time" for two hours on Saturday morning.

"What's this?" she asked Jill.

"Oh, I plan for you to serve me breakfast in bed while I read a book," Jill replied nonchalantly.

"Don't count on it, princess," Mom said.

However, the next morning, Mom surprised Jill with breakfast in bed. "I wanted to help you chill out," Mom said as she put a bamboo tray with juice, eggs, and toast on Jill's bedside table.

Taking time to relax gave Jill the energy she needed.

Positive thought: When I take time to relax, I have more energy to do the things I enjoy.

A Dose of Laughter

Gilbert was down in the dumps. He was recuperating from the chicken pox and could not attend the school Valentine's Day party. To cheer him up, his best friend, Al, brought a funny video movie, two comic books, and a "Peanuts" cartoon over to his house.

Al read and acted out the cartoon for Gilbert. In the cartoon, Snoopy is sick and Charlie Brown has medicine for him. He tells Snoopy that the vet says medicine is good, but laughter is the *best* medicine. Next, he gives Snoopy the medicine. Then he asks his dog which medicine he prefers. Snoopy responds, "HA, HA, HA, HA!"

Al believed that laughter was the best medicine too. He hoped laughing would give Gilbert a lift and help him feel better.

Positive thought: Laughter helps me feel better.

Trusting

Carrie was having a discussion with her dad about letting go of problems.

"Do you trust your bus driver to drive the school bus?" Dad asked.

"Yes," said Carrie.

"Do you trust the lifeguard at the pool to watch over you?"

"Yes," Carrie answered.

"Do you trust the principal to run your school?" Dad continued.

"Of course," Carrie said.

"Then maybe you can trust God with your problems. Figure out what you really need and talk to God about it. God will help you."

Positive thought: I trust God to help me with my problems.

Being Prepared

Al and Robby were the best of friends. They acted so much alike that their moms said the boys were like "two peas in a pod." But there was one very big difference between them. Al was an early bird, and Robby always made it to school just seconds before the last bell rang.

Al would prepare for school the night before. First, he'd choose his outfit. Then he'd pack his lunch. He would also get his books and papers together on his desk so he could pick them up as he left for school.

Robby would rush around in the morning. He would make several trips up and down the steps to the laundry room looking for socks and a clean shirt. Then he'd hurry to make lunch, but discover—too late—that there was no peanut butter, or no bread, or no jelly. And usually as he ran out the door, he'd remember that he'd left a book upstairs in his room, and he would run back to get it.

Preparing for the school day helped Al arrive on time, feeling good. When Robby got to school, his mind and body were still rushing around. It always took time for him to get into a good mood.

Positive thought: Being prepared makes my life easier.

Beauty All Around

"Look at that beautiful red plant," Grandma Annie said to her granddaughter Marie. As she pointed to the plant, something even lovelier landed on Grandma's finger: a butterfly with brown-and-red striped wings.

"That's the most beautiful thing I have ever seen," Marie said. "It's breathtaking."

Grandma and Marie spent the entire afternoon at Callaway Gardens Day Butterfly Center in Pine Mountain, Georgia, taking in all the delights of watching fifty different types of butterflies color the air.

"I don't think I've ever seen so much beauty in one place," Grandma said.

"I know," Marie replied. "My world is filled with beauty today."

Positive thought: I live in a beautiful world. Today I take time to notice that.

Where Does Good Come From?

The Sunday school teacher, Mrs. Ollen, was talking about sowing and reaping, about how what you do comes back to you.

"If you're nice, people will be nice to you," Mrs. Ollen said. "If you're mean and crabby, people will be that way to you."

Brook was having a little problem with this lesson. "There's something I just don't understand," she said to her teacher. "What about when you smile at people and they just look right past you? Or when you go out of your way for a new kid at school, and then that kid treats you like a jerk? If good always comes back to you, how come it doesn't for me?"

Noah, a new student, raised his hand. "Can I answer her please?" he asked. When Mrs. Ollen nodded, Noah continued, "I think that the good things you do and say *will* come back to you, but that you don't always know *when* or from *whom*. It might not be from the person you were nice to. In fact, it might be from someone you never noticed before."

"Have people been nice to you since you moved here?" Mrs. Ollen asked.

"Yes, they really have," Noah answered.

"Were you usually nice to new people at your old school?" the teacher asked.

"Well, I always tried," Noah replied.

"I think Noah has brought home a really good point," Mrs. Ollen said. "What goes around *does* come around—but we don't always know how, when, or where it will appear."

Positive thought: The good I share with others always comes back to me.

Rachael's List

"I've decided what I'm going to be when I grow up," nine-year-old Rachael told her mother one night, "and also what I *never* want to be."

"Why, Rachael, that's great," said her mother. "Tell me."

"I'm either going to be an author, or I'm going to be the person who decides what toys go in cereal boxes," Rachael said.

Her mom smiled.

"I know the last thing sounds a little silly, but I just think it'd be so much fun," Rachael said.

"What do you *not* want to be?" Mom asked.

"An umpire," Rachael—who played third base—said strongly. "When there's a tie, I just don't know how they decide who's safe and who's out. I would hate to have to make that decision all the time."

Positive thought: I can be what I want to be and not be what I don't want to be.

Handling Anger

Kasib asked his uncle Amar to join him in a game of basketball. Kasib had been very angry all afternoon at school, and he wanted to get it out of his system. Dribbling the ball around the driveway and jumping to make those high shots really helped him release that built-up energy.

"Sometimes I feel like I will just explode when I get angry at school," Kasib said to his uncle as he passed the ball to him.

"Keeping cool in school is not the easiest thing to do," Uncle Amar said. "It's a whole different ball game than being able to move around when you're upset.

"I used to make a fist under my desk and pretend I was filling my fist up with all the anger I was feeling. When it got totally full, I would open my hand up just like I was letting the anger go. That helped me until I could go outside and run it off," his uncle said.

Kasib liked the sound of that and decided to try it next time he got upset at school.

"Sounds a lot smarter than fighting with a classmate or arguing with the teacher," Kasib said.

Positive thought: I can find healthy ways to let go of anger.

Teddy Bears in the Classroom

Melinda stared at the floor as she entered her science class and slumped down in her desk. Ms. Dorsey, her science teacher, noticed.

"You look like you need one of these," Ms. Dorsey said as she reached in a box in the closet and held a teddy bear out to Melinda.

Melinda hugged the stuffed animal hard.

"Hey, I want one too," Keith called out.

It surprised Ms. Dorsey when several other members of the junior varsity football team wanted stuffed animals too. Soon most of the class had animals sitting on their desks.

The lesson proceeded as usual, and the students were especially attentive that day.

"Nobody would believe this sight," Ms. Dorsey thought to herself as she gazed around the classroom. "They all look so peaceful holding those animals."

Positive thought: Small things comfort me if I let them.

A Peace Treaty

Kay had been in the same class as her best friend, Margie, from kindergarten through third grade. They even requested the same teacher for fourth grade, and sure enough, both wound up with Mr. Miner.

Only this year, things were different. For the first time, Margie's other good friend, Jo, was in class with Kay and Margie.

"Shoot," said Kay to herself when she saw Jo in Mr. Miner's class on the first day of school. "This is going to be trouble. I just can't stand that Jo. I don't know why, but we always fight."

And it was true. As the year wore on, the fights between Kay and Jo grew worse and worse. When Jo dropped her lunch tray, Kay teased her for days afterward. When Kay wore braids, Jo called her Pippi Longstocking. Poor Margie, good friends to both girls, was always in the middle. The three girls seemed to be stuck, fighting on the playground day after day. *Nobody* liked it.

"I know it's just as much my fault as Jo's," Kay said to herself one day. "I feel like we're at war. This has got to stop."

Kay figured out a plan. She came up with a peace treaty and called Margie and Jo over. Even though Jo stuck her tongue out, Kay held to her plan. "Margie, Jo," she said, "this playground has become a battleground, and we can't go on like this. I propose a truce."

"Jo," she continued, "I want you to know that I am not trying to take Margie from you, and I believe you're not trying to take Margie from me. And I bet we *both* know that Margie's unhappy about this situation. I think that since you and I don't get along, we should take turns playing with Margie at recess."

Margie smiled. "I like it," she said. "I like it a lot."

Jo wasn't so sure. "I have to think about it," she said. But the next day, she agreed. "As long as *I* get to play with Margie first— TODAY," she said.

"Okay," agreed Kay. Secretly, she thought, "How typical. Jo always has to get her way." But they kept the treaty, and it worked. They even found a way to play together, all three of them, on Margie's birthday—for about ten whole minutes.

Positive thought: I can be a peacemaker.

Muscles

Mom was driving her six-year-old son, Chad, and their neighbor Jimbo to school. The boys were in the backseat, bragging to each other about how strong their dads were. But when Mom heard Chad say, "My dad could beat up your dad," she almost drove off the road! Later that day, Mom talked to Chad.

"Chad, have you ever seen your dad hit someone?"

"No," said Chad.

"If you did see him get so angry that he hit someone, would you think he was stronger because he did?" Mom asked.

Chad squirmed, but he didn't say anything.

"Okay. Let's say two fathers catch their sons telling lies. One father hits his son. The other dad is also very mad, but he sits down and talks to his son. Which dad is stronger, Chad?"

"Mom, I was talking about muscles. Using your muscles means you're strong. I'd *like* the second dad better, but that wouldn't mean he's stronger," Chad said.

"Chad, it takes a very strong person to stay calm and not throw their weight around," Mom said.

"Sort of like spiritual muscles?" Chad asked.

"Exactly," Mom said.

Positive thought: I am strong because my spirit is strong.

Standing Up for My Rights

Ross dipped a large corn chip in the warm burrito sauce and chowed down. His uncle remarked how glad he was that Ross had requested this special sauce.

Just then Ross got a disgusted look on his face and said, "Oh gross! What are those people doing smoking at the next table? Aren't we sitting in the nonsmoking section?"

Ross covered his face with his arm and began to complain. "I'm thinking about making a designer oxygen mask so I can breathe when this happens. Maybe those smokers would get it if I did something obvious," he said, raising his voice and glaring at them.

Amazed and a little amused, Ross's uncle asked him when he had started reacting to smoke. Ross said that cigarettes stink and affect his breathing. Plus, in school he had studied the danger of secondhand smoke. "I have a right not to breathe smoky air," Ross said loudly.

Feeling a little embarrassed, Ross's uncle called the waiter over to the table and requested that he ask the couple that was smoking to move into the smoking section. When the waiter approached them, it was obvious that they were embarrassed. They had not realized they were in the nonsmoking section.

Ross's uncle was relieved that they had not heard Ross carrying on.

"Ross," his uncle said, "I agree that breathing smoky air is the pits. But the way you carried on did not do anything to get you a better breathing environment. You were focusing on what you didn't want rather than asking for what you did want."

Positive thought: Asking for what I want helps me more than complaining about what I don't want.

The Good Teacher

Mr. Smith, Lavelle's new teacher, was about fifty years old. And this was his first year of teaching!

One day, Mr. Smith explained to the class that he used to be an engineer for a big company.

"But I always loved children," he said. "So, one day, I decided to go back to school and get trained to be a teacher."

"Isn't that amazing?" Lavelle said to her dad that night. "He almost didn't become a teacher, and now he's everybody's favorite."

"I'm not surprised," said Dad. "When you do what you love, you're usually good at it."

Positive thought: When I do what I love, it shows.

A Second Chance

In May, Doug got a watch for his eleventh birthday. But on the family vacation in June, he left it at the beach by mistake. His father gave him a really bad scolding about it. He told Doug that he would not get another watch until he could take care of one.

Doug felt awful about losing the watch. He didn't know if he would ever get another one. At the same time, though, he wondered, "How will Dad know when I have learned how to take care of a watch if I don't have one to take care of?"

Seven years passed before Doug got another watch. On his high-school graduation day, his dad gave him one.

On the outside Doug looked happy, but on the inside he recalled the hurt he had felt when he lost his first watch.

"I'd have given myself a second chance long before this," he thought to himself.

Positive thought: I give myself a second chance when I make mistakes.

Surviving Resource Class

Lee hurried into the room to avoid being seen. He sat down and tried to catch his breath. Being in resource class meant only one thing to Lee—that he was different. Twice a day, he was separated from his friends. To make matters worse, he was sometimes teased by other students as he entered the resource classroom.

"I wish I could make myself invisible when I come through that door," Lee said. "I'm sick of being teased."

The other resource class students nodded. They knew.

The veins on Douglas's neck bulged as he said, "I got kicked off the football team this quarter 'cause I failed English." He clenched his fist and continued, "Football was the only thing that made school bearable for me."

The room was very quiet for a little while.

"I feel so stupid," Patti said. "I don't see why I can't learn to read like everybody else. It's just not fair."

Ms. Miller, the counselor, listened and understood. She had experienced many of the same feelings because, as a child, she too had been in resource class for a couple of years.

"My brother had a reading problem, and Mom found a reading specialist who helped a lot," Lee told Patti. "Why don't you call my mom and ask her about him?"

"It would be a miracle if he could help me," Patti said. "Thanks for the info."

"I'm sorry you got kicked off the football team, Douglas," Patti said as she patted him on the shoulder. "Maybe when I learn to read better, I could help you in English."

Although the students' problems were not all solved, many of the kids left class in better spirits.

"Sometimes it just helps to talk about what's going on," Lee said to Patti, picking up his book bag to leave.

Positive thought: Talking about my feelings helps me handle my problems better.

Squeaking and Squawking

The bleachers in the gymnasium were filled with parents and friends waiting for the sixth-grade bands to give their first concert. Moms and dads chatted about how they had survived the first few weeks of squeaking and squawking while their children learned to play their instruments.

Each band played its music remarkably well, considering that the players had had their instruments for only three months.

"I enjoyed that!" Ms. Weems said to her son Mel when the concert had ended. "How did you like performing?" she asked.

"I really liked it," Mel said. "It's a neat feeling making a song come alive. I love playing the sax!

"It's sure different from the first week, when I couldn't get a decent sound out of this instrument, isn't it, Mom?" he laughed. "I was really discouraged. The sounds I was making were awful, even to my own ears.

"I'm glad I stuck with it, though," said Mel. "Thanks for not letting me quit, Mom."

Positive thought: When I practice and stick with what I am learning, I will get through the rough spots.

Jump Shot

"There you go again trying to get a jump shot," Carlie called out to her little sister Virginia as she missed the basket. "You never score with a jump shot. Why do you keep trying?"

"I'm doing the best I can," Virginia said. "I wish you would get off my case," she muttered, looking toward the ground.

"Now you've missed a pass!" Carlie yelled, her harsh words punctuated by the ball bouncing on the hard concrete. "We could just end the game right now if you keep that up."

The more Carlie fussed, the more frustrated Virginia became, and instead of playing better she played worse.

"I'm out of here!" Carlie shouted as she stomped off in disgust. "Maybe you should try kickball, little sister."

Feeling low, Virginia dribbled the ball up and down the driveway. She was startled when she heard the sound of bicycle tires stopping behind her.

"Let's shoot some hoops!" her best friend, Amber, called out. "You're warmed up, so you can go first."

As the girls dribbled and shot, other neighborhood kids joined in. They played and played until it started getting dark. There was time for one more play. The score was tied, and Virginia had the ball.

"Go, Virginia!" Amber cheered. "Make that shot. You can do it."

And Virginia did do it. With a smile on her face, she made a beautiful jump shot and scored the winning points.

Positive thought: Focusing on my mistakes makes me make more mistakes. Focusing on the good things I do is always better.

Talking It Over

"C'mon Will," said Kevin. "Your mom isn't even home, so she'll never know you watched this movie. If we don't watch it, I'll go over to somebody else's house where I can watch the kind of movies I want to."

Will looked away angrily.

"Your parents are too strict," Kevin chided. "I think I need some friends who are more grown-up than you."

Worse than the persistent pressure to disobey his parents was the hurt Will felt every time Kevin hinted that he would dump him as a friend. But all this had gone on long enough. Will took a deep breath and got up the courage to speak what he had practiced for a long time.

"Kevin, I don't like it when you push me to disobey my parents. And I *really* don't like it when you threaten not to be my friend anymore just because I won't do what you want.

"I think we can still be friends and can do fun things together. I also think it would be a good idea for you to get some of your other friends to do more of those 'grown-up' things you want to do. Then you can stop bugging me about them," he said.

Will felt as if a million-pound weight had been lifted off his shoulders when he said all that.

Positive thought: Talking things over brings peace of mind.

Telephonitis

"I never thought I would be asking *you* for hints to help me get off the telephone," Marilee said to her teenage sister Ali.

"Yeah, you used to be the one who was always begging *me* to hang up the phone," Ali replied.

"Ali, since I started middle school and met a lot of new friends, it seems like I spend all night on the phone. Sometimes Ellie calls three or four times, and Yvonne always calls at least twice. I don't want to be rude, but I do have a life away from the phone."

"Believe it or not, Marilee, I used to be upset with my friends who had telephonitis too," Ali said. "The hard part was when the same person would call back again and again. What worked for me was saying, 'I really enjoyed talking to you but I have to go now. I have things to do so I won't be able to talk again tonight. Let's meet at your locker tomorrow before school and catch up.'"

"Did your friends think you were a snob?" Marilee asked.

"Actually, I did get some flak at first," said Ali. "But after a few days, they got over it, and we're still friends."

"Thanks for the advice," said Marilee. "I'll try it."

"Well, I hope it helps," said Ali. "I just got a new boyfriend today and I'd like some more phone time!"

Positive thought: I say what I need to say clearly and politely because hinting usually doesn't work.

Enjoying the Good Times

"I'm a little sad about leaving Florida to go home," Tony told his father. "But I have a lot to look forward to when I get back to Georgia. Going to soccer practice and seeing old friends will be fun."

"Well, that's a great attitude," his father said. "I feel the same way. I'm always a little disappointed when our summer vacation ends. I love all the fun things we do as a family—building sand castles, swimming, deep-sea fishing. But I look forward to going back home, too, especially since I'm teaching a brand-new class at the college this fall."

Positive thought: I enjoy the good times I have in my life now, and I look forward to good times to come.

Innermost Feelings

Yesterday, Lindsay made a decision that left her feeling alone. She had been at her friend Julie's house for a sleepover party. She had looked so forward to it—the videos, the fudge brownies, the late-night talks!

But then one of the girls at the party had gotten the bright idea to call girls who weren't invited to the party and tease them. This had happened to Lindsay once, and she had cried for an hour after the call. Lindsay just couldn't do it to someone else. It was too cruel.

Even though she hated feeling alone, Lindsay knew she couldn't go against her own feelings. So she didn't. She spoke up and said she didn't want any part of it. To her relief, Julie had felt the same way and suggested watching a movie instead.

Positive thought: I respect my innermost feelings.

The Inventor

Gerrard couldn't wait to get to the basement workshop and tell his dad the story he'd heard at school about the man who invented *Monopoly*.

Gerrard and his dad shared a hobby. They both liked to invent things. But their creations never got out of the basement. There were always reasons: not enough money for supplies, no time to perfect the creation. And sometimes the inventions just weren't good enough to go public.

"*Monopoly* was invented about sixty years ago during the depression by a man named Charles Darrow," Gerrard said. "The man didn't have much money when he got the idea, but he made it happen anyway. He carved the houses and hotels from scrap lumber."

Dad's face lit up and he nodded as he remembered playing *Monopoly* with the wooden houses and hotels. Gerrard continued, "Mr. Darrow got free paint samples and painted the deed cards by hand and typed them on his typewriter.

"Dad, that game is the most popular game in American history. And the neat thing about it was, Mr. Darrow made it with what he had. He was able to put together two games each day and started selling them to friends and neighbors."

Gerrard's dad sat up straighter, a gleam in his eye. "That's certainly inspiring," he said to his son. "Let's stop thinking of excuses about why we can't make our inventions and instead see what we *can* do to make them."

Positive thought: I begin to create by using what I have.

Full of Love

Have you ever felt full of love for someone, but you just couldn't express it?

Dara felt that way about her fourth-grade teacher, Mr. Stanford. He had a great sense of humor. He loved his students, and they liked to come to class just to be around him.

"I hope he knows how much the kids like him," Dara said to her mom one day. "I'd like to give him a great big hug to show him how great I think he is, but I'd be embarrassed."

"I have a suggestion," her mom said with a smile. "Give him a mental hug. Use your imagination to see yourself giving him a big hug and telling him how much he means to you."

"I like that idea, Mom," Dara said. "I'll do that right now."

Dara closed her eyes and a big smile spread slowly across her face.

Positive thought: Giving mental hugs is a good way to share love.

Friendships

S tan and his cousin Robert were taking turns swinging on the tire swing. As they played, they caught up on old times. Robert was really glad to spend the weekend visiting his favorite cousin. He missed playing with Stan whose dad had gotten transferred to another town.

"I'm glad you're on a baseball team here," he said to Stan. "It's a great way to make friends. The pitcher, James, seems to be your best friend. What makes you like him so much?"

Stan thought for a moment and then replied, "When I tell James good things that are happening with me, he gets happy for me. Most other guys try to come up with something better to top what I've told them.

"I like it that James likes to share my good times and accomplishments even when I've played a better ball game than he has. He is as happy for me as he is for himself!"

Positive thought: A friend is someone who is happy for me.

Expecting Good Things

M om and Dad had invited two couples to spend the weekend at the cabin. It was almost time for them to arrive. Mom sat the children down to explain what she expected of them.

"I expect you to be good this weekend," she said. "What do you think I mean by that?"

"Not being wild," said Bob.

"Being polite," said Gail.

"Not always asking for attention," Autumn added.

"Mom, can I still tell my jokes?" Gail asked, clearly worried. Gail was famous for her silly puns.

"Of course," said Mom. "I'm not asking you not to be yourself. I'm asking you to be your *better* self."

Positive thought: I expect good things of myself. And others know they can expect good things of me too.

People Change

"Visiting the cousins wasn't half as much fun as it used to be," nine-year-old Nina said to her mom as they drove home from their weekend trip to Atlanta. "Cousin Angie talked on the phone for two days, and Deannie read teen magazines."

In the past, the cousins had played together every minute when they visited. The older girls enjoyed playing beauty salon and French-braiding Nina's hair. They made up skits and performed them. Not this time, though. The older girls had paid attention to Nina only when their mom made them.

"As kids get older, they get new and different interests," Mom said. "Your cousins are growing and changing very fast, and sometimes these changes can be hard to take for those around them. It's not personal toward you, although it may feel like it. I'm sorry you didn't have as good a time as before."

Mom waited a few minutes and then laughed as she said, "It's kind of funny. You're too young to play with your teenage cousins, yet you're old enough to play cards with the adults. I sure liked having you as my partner in the canasta games. Grandma has taught you how to play a good game of cards!"

Positive thought: People change as they grow. The changes may affect me, but I choose not to take them personally.

Why Forgive?

Scott's youth group was talking about forgiveness. The counselor asked the boys what they felt like doing when someone made fun of them or told a lie about them.

"Tell everybody I know what a jerk that person is," Scott volunteered.

"Get real mad," said another boy.

"Go over and over in my mind how I really wish I'd told the person off," said another.

"Would you feel sorry for yourself?" the counselor asked.

"You bet," a couple of boys muttered.

"Well, you certainly can do all of these things—and probably will sometimes," said the counselor. "But I wonder if any of these things will make you as happy as forgiving does."

"Happy?" asked Scott. "I don't understand. Forgiving is what you do for someone else, not yourself."

"No, Scott. Forgiving is *for giving*. And the person you're giving to is yourself. And what you're giving yourself is peace of mind."

Positive thought: Forgiving is a choice I make to feel better.

My Most Embarrassing Moment

Ruthie came out of the restroom and ran into the chapel for the wedding rehearsal. She was the junior bridesmaid in her sister's wedding. As she hurried down the aisle to join the wedding party, something felt a little bulky around her waist. She reached behind her and discovered that the skirt of her dress was tucked up in the waist of her panty hose. Her whole backside was exposed!

Ruthie's face turned as bright as a red-hot chili pepper, and her heart pounded. She quickly untucked her dress and looked back to make sure no one was sitting in the pews behind her.

"Thank goodness," she breathed with a sigh of relief. "I don't think I could have gotten through the rehearsal if anyone had seen me," Ruthie said to herself. "This is total embarrassment. The kind you could die from," she muttered.

Ruthie did get through the rehearsal, but it was rough. Every time she thought of the incident, she could feel heat on her face once again.

Positive thought: I can live through embarrassing moments.

Good Fortunes

Sean wanted to give his stepfather, Ron, a really special Christmas present. Sean looked in men's clothing stores and drugstores, but shaving cream and socks weren't what he wanted.

Sean decided he'd have to make the present himself. He wrote a list of things he knew and liked about Ron:

- He's nice to me and Mom.
- He likes Chinese food.
- He's a writer.

Whew! Looking over his list, Sean was beginning to think socks and shaving cream sounded pretty good after all. What could he possibly make for Ron?

Then he got it! Fortunes—like in Chinese fortune cookies! He'd write 365 nice things about Ron and cut them into little strips of paper. Every day, his stepdad could reach into a jar and pull out a good fortune! Sean went to his desk and started writing.

Positive thought: The best gifts are the ones I create myself.

Old Problems

Barry's little sister Amanda was handicapped. Barry was crazy about her—sometimes. She was spunky and never felt sorry for herself because she needed a wheelchair. In fact, she treated it as her "set of wheels" and actually made the other kids jealous that they didn't have one. Barry thought that was really cool.

But other times he was hurt and angry because she seemed to get so much more attention than he did. He knew it wasn't Amanda's fault that she needed a lot of doctor's appointments. But he had missed more than one hockey practice because of her special needs. Maybe everybody has good and bad feelings about people they love, but these feelings made Barry uncomfortable. How could he love Amanda *so* much and still be so angry at her?

Then one day in the library, Barry saw a book displayed on the shelf about having a handicapped brother or sister. Barry read it greedily. When he had finished it, he read it again. It felt so good to know someone else had had his problem. He didn't feel so bad about his feelings anymore.

Although Barry had always loved to read books for fun, he was learning something else about the world of books. Books were useful for helping people learn what they need to learn.

Positive thought: Many problems that are new to me are old to the world. Books can help me get through them.

Body Language

One night while he was working on a science project, Vince looked up *human* in an encyclopedia. There were pages and pages of colorful pictures of the human body—inside and out.

One picture showed the body's many muscles, twisted and twined like a big skein of yarn. Another picture showed the body's organs. There was the liver, which cleans the body like a little vacuum cleaner; the heart, which pumps blood; and the pancreas, which turns food into energy for work and play.

Another page showed the different layers of skin, and still another page illustrated the types of blood cells pumping through the veins and vessels.

Vince couldn't believe all this detail and order. Why, his body was more complicated than the directions for putting together a bicycle. And much more beautiful. So much action, interaction, and connection going on inside of him. It was a miracle.

Positive thought: My body is a miracle.

Getting Pepped Up

The soccer team cheerleaders were having a sleepover party to celebrate the end of the season. They weren't actually official cheerleaders, mind you; they just attended all the neighborhood soccer games and cheered their friends on.

After finishing the pepperoni pizza and soft drinks, the four girls went outside. They all felt a little down now that the season was over.

"I've got it," said Chloe. "Let's make up some cheers. Let's all make up a cheer for each other." The other girls liked the idea.

The group made the first cheer about Chloe since she had come up with the idea. As they cheered for her, they jumped and clapped just as if they were on the field.

> One, her name is Chloe.
> Two, she's really great.
> Three, she knows the score.
> And four, there is lots more!
> Yeah Chloe!

Chloe beamed as her friends performed a personal cheer for her. "I can use this when I need to pep myself up!" she thought.

Positive thought: I cheer myself on when I need pepping up.

Not Fair

"It's not fair!" Randy said. "It's just not fair that Kendall tied with me for first place in the speech contest. I think he spent about an hour writing his speech, and I worked for weeks on mine."

Although Randy was pleased to have done so well himself, he still couldn't believe that someone who had put in so little effort could tie for first place.

As he rode home from the contest, Randy kept muttering about how unfair it was that he had tied with Kendall.

"You know, Randy," his mother said, "you are very talented on the piano. You have played since you were five years old, and you have a natural talent for it. You can listen to a song and play it by ear. Other people would have to work very hard to play as well as you do.

"Maybe Kendall has a natural talent for speeches. I've noticed he does like to talk a lot," she laughed. "Maybe giving speeches is his special talent."

Positive thought: Some talents are natural, and others take work. I appreciate my special talents and those of others.

The Checkered Sunglasses

During a shopping trip at the mall, eight-year-old Sondra was selecting a pair of sunglasses. She had narrowed it down to a pair of hot-pink ones or a blue-and-white checkered pair.

She held up both for her mother to see. "I really like the blue ones," she said. "But the pink ones are two dollars less. Which do you think I should buy, Mom?"

"I think you should buy what you really want," Mom said.

Sondra's heart beat a little faster as she thought about the idea of getting what she really wanted—instead of what was the best deal.

"Okay, I've decided," she said as she took the checkered glasses to the checkout counter.

Mom could tell Sondra had made the right decision by the big smile on her daughter's face.

Positive thought: It's okay to have what I really want.

Tug-of-War

Wayne went to his older brother Malvin for advice on how to handle a situation involving two of his good friends. Wayne's friends had been fighting for days, and they wanted him to take sides.

Malvin had experience in this area, so he was a good person to ask. "First, you have to work with your own self about this problem," he told Wayne.

"Keep telling yourself that this is not *your* argument," he continued. "Then see if you can say something to both boys about how you feel. This works for me most of the time.

"I would tell my friends that I liked both of them but that I did not want to get into their argument. A couple of times they turned it around and got mad at *me*. That was rough for a little bit. But we always stayed friends after it blew over.

"It takes courage not to get into someone else's fight and even more courage to say, 'I like you, but I won't take sides.'" Malvin paused and looked at Wayne for a moment.

"But you know," he continued, "you're a courageous kid. And I know you can do it."

Positive thought: I have the courage not to take sides in my friends' arguments.

Chopsticks

Don did not want to practice the piano. He preferred to be outside playing with friends. He gazed out the window as he banged chopsticks on the white keys. Hoping the awful sounds would irritate his mom, he played the clashing notes louder and louder.

Finally, the noise started bothering *him,* so he decided to play something different. Don began playing some popular sheet music his teacher had lent him. Soon he was completely absorbed in his practice. The piano sang as he played a classical piece, Chopin's *Polonaise.*

After a while, his mom interrupted him and told him he could play outside. Don couldn't believe he had played for forty-five minutes. He had gotten so involved that he actually practiced fifteen minutes extra.

Positive thought: Becoming involved in what I have to do can turn a task into a treat.

Listening Helps

"I don't know what to do to help Bonnie," Barb said to her mom. "I thought when school started, she would feel better, but the first week of classes was really hard on her. A lot of kids hadn't heard that her mom died during the summer. When *that* got around, everyone started asking questions. Sometimes I see her in the hall with a glassy look in her eyes. I know she's fighting back tears.

"Will she be sad for the rest of her life, Mom? How could she be happy again knowing her mom will never be back?" Barb paused and wiped back a tear of her own. "I'm afraid to say much to her about her mom because I'm afraid I'll upset her and make her cry," Barb confided.

"Letting Bonnie know you care and listening to her are the best things you can do for her," said Mom. "And she may cry, but it's not because you have upset her. She just has a lot of tears. In time, Bonnie will be happy again."

"My throat feels tight every time I think about it," Barb confided, "but it helps me to talk to you."

Positive thought: I can help by listening.

Sometimes It's Tough!

A nna sat in her room trying to do her homework. She was having a rough time. Her attention was on something that had happened at school, not on her studies. The words *blimp, chubby,* and *fatso* rang in her ears as she recalled scenes from gym class.

"Why did I do it?" she thought out loud. "Why did I participate in making fun of Nolan? He's a nice guy. There's just a lot more of him than most kids our age."

Although she had not called Nolan any names, she had been with the girls who teased him. The pull to be a part of the group was much stronger than the urge to do what was right. Anna gave in, and she was paying for it now. She was feeling guilty for not speaking up. She really wished she had found the courage to ask her friends not to tease Nolan anymore. Anna wondered if the other girls felt this way too.

"The next time I start to make fun of someone, I am going to think about how bad I feel afterward. I'll also think about how I would feel if I were the one being picked on. Hopefully, that will be enough to keep me out of it," she thought.

Positive thought: Sometimes it's tough standing up for what I feel is right. I am learning to be strong enough to do it.

Bad Things

Mom and eleven-year-old Doug had just finished watching the news on TV. It had been pretty depressing.

"Mom," Doug said, struggling for just the right words. "Where do bad things come from?"

"You know that's really a deep question, don't you?" Mom asked.

Doug nodded.

"Well, some people think *we* cause the bad that comes to us. Some think that there's a force of evil. Other people think that evil is caused by fear—maybe *is* fear with a scary face on it."

"What do *you* think, Mom?" Doug persisted.

"I'm not always sure *what* I think, Doug. But the main thing I *do* know is that bad never comes from God. God is the power for good. God will not harm you or do bad things to you.

"I believe that God wants only good for us."

Positive thought: God wants only good for me.

Inside/Outside

For as long as Ashley could remember, people had made fun of her classmate Barbie.

"She's wearing the same jeans *again*," her classmates teased.

"Her hair—doesn't she *ever* brush it?" was another comment.

Barbie was really thin, and her dirty blonde hair was so bushy that it made her head look too big for her body. All Barbie's outward features led someone to unkindly nickname her "Barbie Doll," and the name had stuck.

One Saturday morning, Ashley bumped into Barbie at the library. Barbie was returning a book that Ashley had just loved reading. The two girls started talking about it, and Ashley realized that she and Barbie had a lot in common.

Suddenly—and sadly—Ashley realized how much more there was to Barbie than just her looks.

Positive thought: To know someone on the inside, I need to see past the outside.

Show-and-Tell at Camp

Denton, the tall, athletic counselor at camp, was giving the daily announcements in the mess hall after lunch .

After handing out the much-awaited letters from home, Denton told the campers, "Tonight, bring something special to the campfire sing-along. We're each going to share something really special with the others."

Julie Anne had no trouble deciding what she would share. That night, when Denton called for volunteers, she marched up to the circle. She was holding a grey, bedraggled teddy bear. Its fur was covered with little fuzzy balls, like an old sweater.

"This is my Teddy," she said, holding him up proudly. "He goes everywhere I go. He is my favorite thing in the world because I can tell him anything, and he doesn't ever tell anyone!"

Positive thought: I can find a trusted someone—or something—to share my secrets with.

The Spelling Bee

Erin felt so foolish. She had completely forgotten to do an assignment her new teacher, Mrs. Stickney, had given the class.

To make matters worse, it was an art project—not hard at all—and would have been fun to do.

"Now Mrs. Stickney is going to think I'm one of those kids who don't do their homework," Erin said to her parents that night. "And she probably thinks I'm not good at art either. Oh, darn it. How *could* I have forgotten?"

"Wait a minute," said Dad. "Erin, remember Mrs. Stickney will be your teacher for the rest of the year. You're acting as if you won't get a second chance with her. You will."

"You really think so, Dad?" Erin asked.

"I really do, Erin," Dad said. "Life's not a spelling bee, where you're out if you make one error. Life constantly gives us chances to correct our mistakes."

Positive thought: I get more than one chance.

What's Weird

Charlotte and Heather both picked their favorite kind of cereal to eat for breakfast. Charlotte's mouth hung open as she watched Heather pour apple juice over her cereal.

"You're weird," Charlotte said to Heather. "Why are you having juice instead of milk on your cereal?"

"I don't like milk, but I do like cereal," Heather replied. "One day I discovered that apple juice on cereal tastes just fine, as long as the cereal doesn't have lots of sugar in it."

"Yuck!" said Charlotte, wrinkling her nose.

"Just because my tastes are different from yours doesn't mean I am weird," said Heather. "It means I'm an individual."

Heather dug her spoon in and took a big bite of cereal. "Mmmmmmmm," she said, smiling at Charlotte. "Tastes very good."

Positive thought: It's okay to like things that are different from what my friends like.

Who Says?

"Did you get one of the free passes the bus driver gave out Friday?" Brooke asked her friend Murray as they rode to the newspaper meeting at school early Monday morning.

"No, I didn't!" said Murray in a huff. "The bus driver only gave them to girls. She thinks all boys misbehave. I don't act up on the bus, and I can't help it if my assigned seat is next to the biggest behavior problem at school.

"I deserved one of those passes. In fact, it made me so mad, look what I wrote," Murray said. He pulled out a long sheet of computer papers. Written in two-inch black letters were these words:

Who says boys can't behave?
Who says boys act worse than girls?
Who says boys always get in trouble?
You do!
And it's just not true!

"I felt better after I wrote this," Murray said. "I'd like to pin this printout on my back and drag it around school all day to protest, but I guess that would be too close to misbehaving," he said with a grin.

Positive thought: I have a right to be angry when people judge me by what sex I am and not by who I am.

One Thought at a Time

"**C**lose your eyes," the guidance counselor, Mr. Harris, instructed the group of fourth graders. "Now tell me. How many thoughts can you think at a time?" he asked.

Some children were squinting their eyes tightly. Others were wrinkling their noses. You could almost see the wheels of their minds turning.

"I tried and I tried, but I was only able to think one thought at a time," Paul said. The other children nodded in agreement.

"That's right," Mr. Harris said. "We can think only one thought at a time. Sometimes it may seem as if we think a lot of thoughts at a time because thoughts come very quickly."

The group decided to use what they learned to make up a special thought for the week: "I can think only one thought at a time, so I will make it a positive one."

Positive thought: I can think only one thought at a time, so I choose to think a positive one.

Mixed Emotions

Robin and Shannon chatted away about the fun things they could do once Robin moved into the city. Robin's dad had gotten a new job, and their family was moving.

"I'll be so glad when you live near me," Shannon said. "Now I'll get to see you more often than just on Sundays."

"We can have sleepovers and maybe we'll even go to the same school!" Robin said.

Shannon's mind raced as she thought about how nice it would be to have Robin within biking distance. They could go on picnics and swimming in the park next summer. Shannon chattered on about the possibilities until she noticed Robin looking sad.

"Why the sad face, Robin?" Shannon asked, still caught up in her own excitement.

"Because I *am* sad, Shannon. It feels really weird to know something that brings a lot of happiness also brings sadness. I especially don't want to leave my school chorus group. I was accepted into the advanced group for next year, and now I won't be able to be in it.

"Feeling happy and sad at the same time is really odd," Robin said.

Positive thought: Mixed emotions can feel odd. It helps to talk about them.

The Box Turtle

Preston settled down on the newly mown grass at Camp High Harbor, the sun hot on his face. As he cracked open his new mystery book, he noticed, out of the corner of his eye, a box turtle moving slowly toward the seawall that edged much of Lake Burton.

Caught up in his book, Preston was startled to hear a *kerplunk*. The turtle had jumped—or fallen—into the water. Knowing that box turtles are land turtles and don't usually swim, Preston was surprised to see the turtle swimming toward the diving pier.

Soon, the turtle was scratching against the pier, trying to gain a foothold. There was no way it could get out. Preston walked out on the pier, picked up the little creature, and carried it back to dry land.

The turtle stared, unblinking, at Preston for a long time. Then it slowly ambled off toward the woods.

"Well, I did *my* good deed for the day," Preston thought, feeling very pleased with himself for having helped a fellow creature.

Positive thought: My pleasure in giving can be the only thank-you I need.